One Little Teddy Bear

Mark Burgess

VIKING

One little teddy bear
Looking for his shoe;
Look inside the clothes cupboard,
Now there are . . .

Two little teddy bears
Underneath a tree;
Look up in the branches,
Now there are . . .

Three little teddy bears
Dancing on the floor;
Look behind the curtain,
Now there are . . .

Four little teddy bears
Going for a drive;
Open *up the sunroof*,
Now there are . . .

Five little teddy bears
Doing magic tricks;
Look inside the magic box,
Now there are . . .

Six little teddy bears
Looking up to heaven;
Lift the red umbrella,
Now there are . . .

Seven little teddy bears
Trying hard to skate;
Look behind the holly bush,
Now there are . . .

Eight little teddy bears
Sitting down to dine;
Lift up the tablecloth,
Now there are . . .

Nine little teddy bears
Nearly home again;
Look inside the front door,
Now there are . . .